DO ANTS WEAR PANTS?

by
Gabrielle Grice

Do Ants Wear Pants ©2020 Gabrielle Grice

Illustrator—Alland Wijaya
(radenalanwijaya@gmail.com)

All other images ©2020 Gabrielle Grice

To William—my number one fan!

Do bears sit in chairs?

Do skunks
play in trunks?

Do otters play on teeter-totters?

Do turtles jump hurdles?

Do storks eat with forks?

Do fishes make wishes?

Do hares travel in pairs?

Do cows have eyebrows?

Do hogs wear clogs?

Do bees have knees?

Do kangaroos read the news?

Do antelopes eat cantaloupes?

Do birds
say words?

Do cats wear hats?

Do crocodiles
walk for miles?

Do parrots
eat carrots?

Do doves wear gloves?

Do foxes
sleep in boxes?

Do goats
ride in boats?

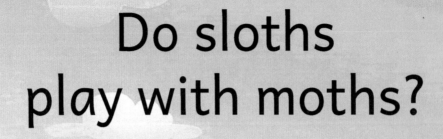

Do sloths play with moths?

Do peacocks
wear socks?

Do porcupines
read signs?

Do seals do cartwheels?

Do sharks play in parks?

Do crabs drive cabs?

Do snakes eat cakes?

Wasn't that so much fun? Which question was your favorite one?

About the Author

Gabrielle Grice is a retired police officer, who writes adult books under another pen name.

She lives with her two dogs, Boomer and Bella, who love to cuddle while their mom creates stories.

RIP Jinx (2010-2020)

Made in the USA
Las Vegas, NV
08 February 2024

85503245R00029